CRESSMAN
LIBRARY

CEDAR CREST
COLLEGE

Presented by:

Anna B. Steckel

First published in the United States, Great Britain, Canada,
Australia and New Zealand in 1992 by North-South Books,
an imprint of Nord-Süd Verlag AG, Gossau Zürich, Switzerland

Distributed in the United States by North-South Books Inc.

Library of Congress Cataloging-in-Publication Data
Moers, Hermann.
[Hugo und sein kleiner Bruder. English]
Hugo's baby brother/by Hermann Moers: illustrated by Józef
Wilkoń: translated by Rosemary Lanning.
Translation of: Hugo und sein kleiner Bruder.
Summary: Hugo the young lion, although fully grown, resents
sharing his mother's attention with his new baby brother.
ISBN 1-55858-137-5 (trade)
ISBN 1-55858-146-4 (lib. bdg.)
[1. Lions—Fiction.   2. Brothers—Fiction.   3. Babies—Fiction.
4. Mother and child—Fiction.]   I. Wilkoń, Józef, ill.   II. Title.
PZ7.H7215Hv   1991
[E]—dc20   91-7775

British Library Cataloguing in Publication Data
Moers, Hermann, *1930—*
Hugo's baby brother.
I. Title   II. [Hugo und sein kleiner Bruder. *English*]
833.914   [J]
ISBN 1-55858-137-5

1 3 5 7 9 10 8 6 4 2
Printed in Belgium

Hugo's Baby Brother

By Hermann Moers
Illustrated by Józef Wilkoń

Translated by Rosemary Lanning

North-South Books

NEW YORK

Hugo was no longer a cub, but a strong young lion. He had a full set of fine, sharp teeth, and his mother had taught him all he needed to know.

Then, one morning, Hugo saw a newborn cub tottering around his mother, crying for milk.

"This is Sasha, your new brother," she told Hugo.

"I haven't got a brother," said Hugo indignantly. "I've always been your only son."

"That was so," said his mother with a smile, "but now I have two cubs to look after."

Hugo walked away in a huff. He didn't like the idea of his mother caring for someone else.

"If I do something really terrible," he thought, "she'll see that I'm the one who needs looking after." He reached out for a poisonous snake.

Luckily his father saw what he was doing and roared, "Hugo, don't be so stupid!"

Hugo went and hid in the tall grass. He was ashamed of himself for acting so stupidly. Then his friend Helen came running past. She was surprised when she saw Hugo. "What are you doing there?" she asked.

"Hiding," growled Hugo, "and I'm never coming out."

"That sounds boring," laughed Helen. "Come on, let's play cat and mouse. I'll be the mouse."

Hugo's bad mood disappeared at once. "All right," he said, leaping out at Helen. "Here I come!"

When the game was finished Hugo went back to his mother and found her gently licking little Sasha.

Hugo limped towards her moaning. "Ooh! Ow! That hurts."

"Have you stepped on a thorn?" asked his mother. She looked at his paw and then laughed. "Oh Hugo," she sighed, "you're making it up. There's nothing wrong with you."

"It hurts, all the same," he insisted, gazing at her with a pitiful expression.

"I'll make it better for you," said his mother kindly.

"All right," said Hugo, happy again. That night the three of them went to sleep piled up like a soft, warm heap of pillows.

Hugo's mother was delighted that her two sons were friends at last. But as soon as little Sasha woke there was trouble again.

Sasha was trying to catch his own tail, but he was much too clumsy. Hugo snapped at Sasha's tail and held it between his teeth.

Sasha howled with pain and woke their mother who cuffed Hugo on the ear.

"I was only trying to help the silly creature catch his tail!" grumbled Hugo. He walked away thinking how unfair it all was.

Mother carried Sasha on her back while Hugo trotted along behind. "Will you carry me now?" asked Hugo in a babyish voice.

"No, you're much too big. You could almost carry *me!*" laughed his mother.

"That's not true," whimpered Hugo. "I'm only little, and it's time for my milk."

His mother turned and nibbled his ear tenderly. "You are big and strong, but you'll always be my dear little Hugo," she said.

"Oh good," said Hugo, cheering up. "Then I'll go and play with the other lions."

Towards evening the lions started to feel hungry. As always, the mothers ran ahead to scout for prey. The strong male lions with their magnificent manes were in no hurry to join them.

Hugo's place was in the middle of the pride with the other young lions, but when night came he ran back to his mother. He liked to know she was there to protect him even though he was big and strong enough to look after himself.

Hugo took his mother's tail between his teeth as he had always done as a baby. He tried to be very gentle so that she wouldn't notice.

She did notice, of course, but said nothing.

Sasha was pleased to see his mother again next morning.
"Watch me!" he said as he tried to pounce on a lizard.
"What a brave little fellow!" said mother, encouragingly.
"Huh!" snorted Hugo in disgust. "I'm ten times braver than
that little weakling." He ran off and tried to jump on a buffalo
which immediately threw him to the ground. The angry buffalo
lowered its powerful head with its dangerous horns.

Mother ran to rescue Hugo. She knew that he was jealous because she had praised Sasha. "You are the bravest lion in the whole pride," she said, nuzzling Hugo, "but promise never to do anything so dangerous again."

"I promise," said Hugo.

Later the lions met for a delicious meal. Sasha leapt up at his big brother and tried to snatch meat from his mouth.

"Go away, little one," growled Hugo, but Sasha wouldn't let go.

Hugo decided to teach his baby brother to treat him with more respect. "Watch me," he said. "I'm going to show you how a big lion catches a zebra."

Hugo leapt onto a branch that was as high as a zebra's back. The branch snapped and Hugo tumbled to the ground.

"Where's the zebra?" said Sasha innocently.

"Forget it," growled Hugo, shaking the dust from his fur.

After their meal all the lions lay around dozing. Sasha was the only one who didn't feel like resting.

"Let's have a fight!" he yelled playfully, jumping on his brother.

"I'll teach you not to spoil my afternoon nap!" growled Hugo. He grabbed Sasha by the scruff of his neck and shook him. Then he picked him up by his tail and boxed his ears. "Have you had enough, yet?" he said fiercely.

Sasha gulped, then glared at his brother. "Just wait until I'm bigger," he growled. "Then I'll make mincemeat of you."

The lions went to drink at a water hole. Sasha, who had never seen so many animals before, stared at them wide-eyed. He trotted up to an elephant to have a closer look at its trunk, but the elephant got very annoyed. It trumpeted loudly and raised one giant foot to squash the inquisitive little creature.

Hugo swiftly scooped up his brother and carried him to safety. "I can't take my eyes off you for one minute," he said.

Mother was grateful to Hugo for rescuing her baby. She rubbed her head on Hugo's shoulder. Hugo gently shrugged off his mother's caress.

"He's my brother, isn't he?" he said as he walked back to the pride. But before he went he turned and winked at little Sasha.

J F M694h

Moers, Hermann

Hugo's baby brother

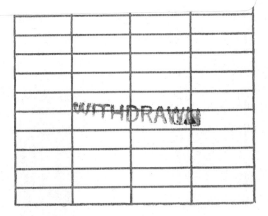